Merlin

The Magical Puppy

MERLIN ON ICE

KEITH LITTLER

CARLTON
BOOKS

It was a bitterly cold day in Sandybay. Everybody was wrapped up in their warmest clothes.

Merlin the puppy and Mr Crabtree were watching Mr Pickles fishing.

Mr Crabtree shivered. "The pond in my garden has frozen over," he said.

Mr Pickles laughed. "I've seen colder weather than this." But when he looked at the fish dangling on the end of his fishing line, he realized it was frozen solid.

Merlin saw his friend Kizzie out walking with Miss Parkway.

"Hi, Kizzie," he barked as he wagged his tail. Merlin was always happy to see Kizzie.

"They say it might snow tomorrow," Kizzie told him. "I heard some people in the shop say they will go ice-skating if the harbour freezes."

Merlin had never seen ice and snow before. "Oh, I hope it does snow tomorrow," he barked. "Then we can go ice-skating too!"

But like all little puppies, Merlin did not want to wait – he wanted to skate now.

Then he had an idea. He would use his magic collar. The problem was that Merlin could never remember how to make his collar work.

He closed his eyes and concentrated very hard. "I want to go skating with Kizzie now!" he barked hopefully.

Nothing happened.

"Oh, I wish I could go ice-skating with Kizzie," Merlin whined.

As soon as he said the magic word, "wish", his collar began to glow and sparkle.

Suddenly Merlin was standing in the middle of a large frozen lake. The snow was white and glistened like diamonds and the ice was shiny like a mirror. It was magical!

"This is wonderful!" Merlin barked happily.

But when he tried to take a step his paws slipped on the ice and he nearly fell over.

"Oh, this is difficult," he whined.

He tried another step and almost fell over once again.

Poor Merlin thought he was going to be stuck in the middle of the lake for ever.

At that moment Kizzie skated gracefully by. Merlin was really pleased to see her.

"Help! I'm stuck!" he yelped, wobbling on the slippery ice.

"Don't worry," Kizzie said. "Follow me and I'll teach you how to skate."

Merlin slithered this way and that, but he wasn't very good. To make matters worse, Oscar the cat suddenly whooshed by.

"Hi, Kizzie," he purred. "Would you like to skate with me?"

"Just a minute," Merlin barked. "Kizzie is skating with me!"

Oscar laughed. "But you don't know how to skate!" Then he rolled up his tail and gave Merlin a big push.

Merlin slid all the way across the lake until he hit the bank and fell into a big pile of snow.

Gull fluttered down beside him. "You're not going to let Oscar push you around, are you?" he squawked.

"It's no use," Merlin sighed. "I wish I could skate like a champion in a competition, then I would show that silly cat."

As soon as Merlin said the magic word, "wish", his collar began to glow and sparkle.

Merlin skated out on to the ice, balancing perfectly.

"Excuse me," he barked to Oscar. "I want to skate with Kizzie now."

Kizzie smiled at Merlin. "Yes, I think it is Merlin's turn," she said.

"He's clumsy and he can't skate," Oscar purred, "so be careful he doesn't stand on your paws."

But Merlin wasn't clumsy now, thanks to his magic collar.

Merlin and Kizzie skated together around the ice like true champions. All the people watching were very impressed.

"How did you become such a great ice-skater?" Kizzie asked.

"Oh, just practice," Merlin barked.

He then grabbed Kizzie's tail and spun her round and round.

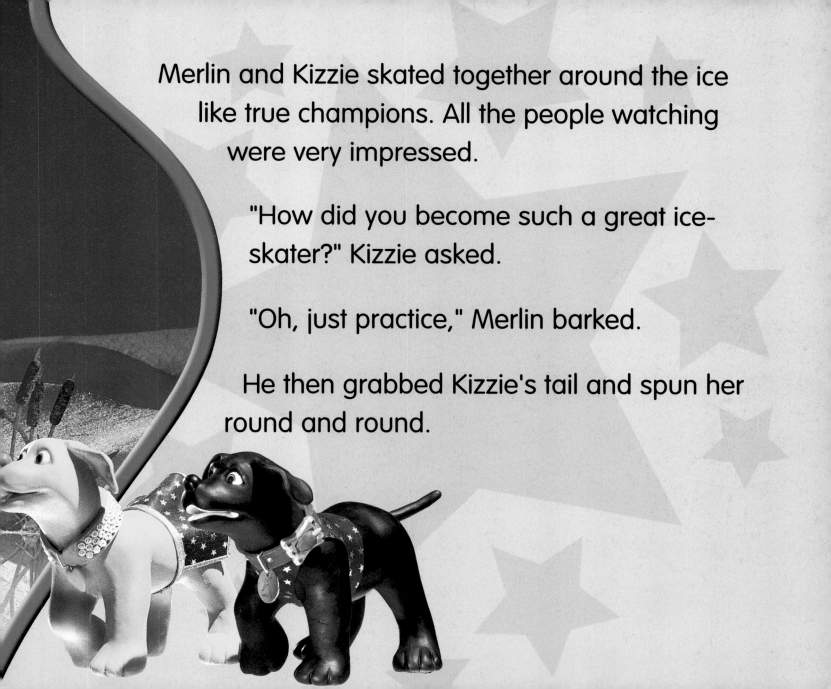

"Wheee!" Kizzie laughed.

But Merlin accidentally let go and Kizzie flew straight into the crowd.

With a loud crash and lots of shouting, they all fell in a big heap.

"Uh-oh," Merlin barked. "I could be in big trouble now. I wish I was safely back home."

As soon as he said the magic word, "wish", his collar began to glow and sparkle.

Suddenly the frozen lake vanished.

"Phew," Merlin barked happily. "I made it."

Ernie was pleased to see him.

"Ah, Merlin, there you are. I've heard it might snow tomorrow. We can go ice-skating."

Merlin hung his head. "Oh, that's all right. I think I've had quite enough of ice and snow for one day, thank you."